All Aboard!

Our Trip

STOP-n-GO RAILWAY

SCHEDULE

Train 23 ✳ Big Lake to Corndale

THURSDAY	Big Lake, ME	Depart	5:30 P.M.
	Snow Bank, NH	Arrive	7:30 P.M.
		Depart	8:00 P.M.
	Middleton, MA	Arrive	10:00 P.M.
		Depart	10:15 P.M.
FRIDAY	Herdville, VA	Arrive	11:45 A.M.
		Depart	12:30 P.M.
	Tempus, NC	Arrive	3:30 P.M.
		Depart	5:30 P.M.
	Fugit, SC	Arrive	8:00 P.M.
		Depart	9:00 P.M.
SAT	Corndale, FL	Arrive	10:30 A.M.

Change trains for Sunny City! ☀

Train 24 ✳ Corndale to Blue Water

SATURDAY	Corndale, FL	Depart	3:30 P.M.
	Sunny City, FL	Arrive	4:45 P.M.
		Depart	5:00 P.M.
	Blue Water, FL	Arrive	6:00 P.M.

by Daphne Skinner
Illustrated by Jerry Smath

Kane Press, Inc.
New York

To Jill Rosenberg Smath,

—JS

Library of Congress Cataloging-in-Publication Data

Skinner, Daphne.
     All aboard! / by Daphne Skinner ; illustrated by Jerry Smath.
        p.   cm. — (Math matters.)
     Summary: When Kit, Jay, and their grandma take a train trip across the country, Kit learns the importance of being on time.
     ISBN-13: 978-1-57565-239-9 (alk. paper)
     ISBN-10: 1-57565-239-0 (alk. paper)
        [1. Railroads—Trains—Fiction. 2. Voyages and travels—Fiction. 3. Punctuality—Fiction.]   I. Smath, Jerry, ill. II. Title.
     PZ7.S6277Ak 2007
     [E]—dc22
                                                                    2006026410

10 9 8 7 6 5 4 3 2 1

First published in the United States of America in 2007 by Kane Press, Inc.
Printed in Hong Kong.

MATH MATTERS is a registered trademark of Kane Press, Inc.

www.kanepress.com

"All aboard!" the conductor shouted.

Jay and Kit raced down the platform and climbed on—just before the train chugged off.

"That was close!" said their grandma. "I was afraid I'd have to go to Florida all alone!"

Jay looked at Kit. "Can't you *ever* be on time?"

Kit laughed. "Time *shmime!*" she said.

Gram loved trains, so they were all taking the Stop-n-Go Railway to Cousin Jo's wedding.

Jay got to the roomette first. "Cool!" he said.

"Look how the beds fold out of the wall," said Kit. "It's like magic."

Jay checked his new waterproof calendar watch. "We're on schedule," he said. "We'll be at the Happy Cow in about sixteen hours."

Gram, Kit, and Jay had each chosen a place to visit on their trip. The Happy Cow was Jay's. "The train only stops for 45 minutes," he said. "So our timing has to be perfect, Kit."

Kit wasn't listening. Jay sighed and picked up the menu. "Hey, the dining car is open!"

"You two go ahead," said Kit. "I'll catch up."

"Uh huh." Jay knew she'd be late.

STOP-n-GO RAILWAY
Train 23 ✻ Big Lake to Corndale

T H U R S D A Y	Big Lake, ME	Depart	5:30 P.M.
	Snow Bank, NH	Arrive	7:30 P.M.
		Depart	8:00 P.M.
	Middleton, MA	Arrive	10:00 P.M.
		Depart	10:15 P.M.
F R I D A Y	Herdville, VA	Arrive	11:45 A.M.
		Depart	12:30 P.M.
	Tempus, NC	Arrive	3:30 P.M.
		Depart	5:30 P.M.
	Fugit, SC	Arrive	8:00 P.M.
		Depart	9:00 P.M.
S A T	Corndale, FL	Arrive	10:30 A.M.

Train 24 ✻ Corndale to Blue Water

S A T U R D A Y	Corndale, FL	Depart	3:30 P.M.
	Sunny City, FL	Arrive	4:45 P.M.
		Depart	5:00 P.M.
	Blue Water, FL	Arrive	6:00 P.M.

Kit was late a lot. She was late for
soccer games. She was late for trick or
treating. One time, she was even late for
her own birthday party!

HAPPY BIRTHDAY, KIT!

And she was late getting to dinner. When she finally strolled in, Jay was already on dessert.

Gram gave Kit a menu. "Remember, kids," she said, "the train won't stop long in Herdville tomorrow. If we dawdle, we'll never get to the Happy Cow."

"No problem!" Jay said.

"Whatever," said Kit.

		Arrive	11:45 A.M.
F **R** **I** **D** **A** **Y**	**Herdville,** **VA**	Arrive	11:45 A.M.
		Depart	12:30 P.M.
	Tempus, **NC**	Arrive	3:30 P.M.
		Depart	5:30 P.M.
	Fugit, **SC**	Arrive	8:00 P.M.
		Depart	9:00 P.M.

The next morning, Jay woke Kit up extra early. He knew she wouldn't notice. She never looked at clocks.

When the train stopped in Herdville, he rushed Gram and Kit to the bus stop.

The bus pulled up at 11:50, and they got to the Happy Cow at 12:00. *Perfect timing!*

SWEET ST.

12:00

HAPPY COW

JAY'S
HAPPY COW
SCHEDULE

Train arrives in Herdville: 11:45 A.m.
Bus departs train station: 11:50 A.m.
Bus arrives at Happy Cow: 12:00 P.m.
Bus departs Happy Cow: 12:15 P.m.
Bus arrives at train station: 12:25 P.m.
Train departs Herdville: 12:30

Jay ordered a Fast-Track Fudge milkshake at 12:05. Grandma ordered her Blueberry-Gingko Memory Waker at 12:07.

But Kit just couldn't make up her mind. "Kiwi-Grape?" she wondered out loud. "Banana-Mango? Peppermint-Pear . . . ?"

Kit took so long that they almost missed the bus back to the station.

Then the bus got caught in traffic, and they had to run for their train.

"That was *way* too close!" panted Jay.

"It was my one chance to have a Happy Cow shake," Kit said. "I had to pick just the right flavor." She took a big slurp. "Double-Berry Slow-Melt Brain Freezer—yum."

That afternoon was Kit's big stop.

Her favorite magicians, Hector and Bob, were performing in Tempus, North Carolina. The train was stopping there to pick up new passengers. So Gram, Kit, and Jay had just enough time to see the 4:00 magic show.

		Arrive	11:45 A.M.
F	**Herdville, VA**	Depart	12:30 P.M.
R		Arrive	3:30 P.M.
I	**Tempus, NC**	Depart	5:30 P.M.
D		Arrive	8:00 P.M.
A **Y**	**Fugit, SC**	Depart	9:00 P.M.

When they got off the train, Gram looked up and down the street. "The taxi was supposed to be here at 3:30."

"Well, where is it?" asked Kit nervously.

"It's late," said Jay.

"What if we miss the show?" Kit cried.

TEMPUS THEATER
Presents
HECTOR and BOB'S
MAGICAL MAGIC
EXTRAVAGANZA!
• Two Days Only •
Thursday, March 6
12:00 2:00 4:00
Friday, March 7
12:00 2:00 4:00 6:00

TAXI

The taxi finally showed up. "Sorry I'm late," said the driver. "I'm behind schedule today."

Kit scrambled inside. Jay had never seen her move so fast.

Every time they stopped for a light, Kit bounced up and down and whispered, "Hurry up! Hurry up!"

They got to their seats just as Hector and Bob were doing their first trick.

Hector sawed Bob in half.

Bob pulled a scarf out of Hector's nose.

Hector changed Bob into a gorilla.

Bob changed Hector into a whirling cloud that smelled like grape juice.

Then Hector asked for volunteers. Kit's arm shot up—and he chose her!

Up on the stage, Kit held a top hat as Hector pulled out a rabbit, a clock, and a pink feather boa. It was like a wonderful dream.

Hector and Bob gave Kit the boa, the clock, and their new book, *Timing is Everything*. She practically fainted.

"That was cool!" Jay said on the way back. Kit was still in a happy daze. "I wouldn't have missed it for anything," she said. Then she remembered. She almost *had* missed it. Maybe timing *is* everything, Kit thought.

That night, Kit was right on time for dinner.
Jay checked his watch. "You're *ready?*"
Kit just smiled.

"Better be on time tomorrow, you two," Gram
said. "Don't forget—we're switching trains."

"Right," said Jay. "We get to Corndale at 10:30
and find lockers for our
bags. And then we visit
your special stop!"

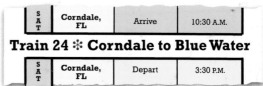

S A T	Corndale, FL	Arrive	10:30 A.M.

Train 24 ✻ Corndale to Blue Water

S A T	Corndale, FL	Depart	3:30 P.M.

The next day, Kit was right on time again. They pulled into Corndale at exactly 10:30 and caught the State Fair Trolley at 11:00.

The fair was huge! There were rides, and games, and five cotton candy booths—but Gram's mind was on just one thing. "Let's head right over to the Giant Vegetables," she said. "I hear they're amazing!"

GREAT STATE FAIR
TROLLEY SCHEDULE
Monday–Friday

Departs Station	Arrives at Fair		Departs Fair	Arrives at Station
9:00 A.M.	9:30 A.M.			
11:00 A.M.	11:30 A.M.		9:30 A.M.	10:00 A.M.
1:00 P.M.	1:30 P.M.		11:30 A.M.	12:00 A.M.
3:00 P.M.	3:30 P.M.		1:30 P.M.	2:00 P.M.
5:00 P.M.	5:30 P.M.		3:30 P.M.	4:00 P.M.
			5:30 P.M.	6:00

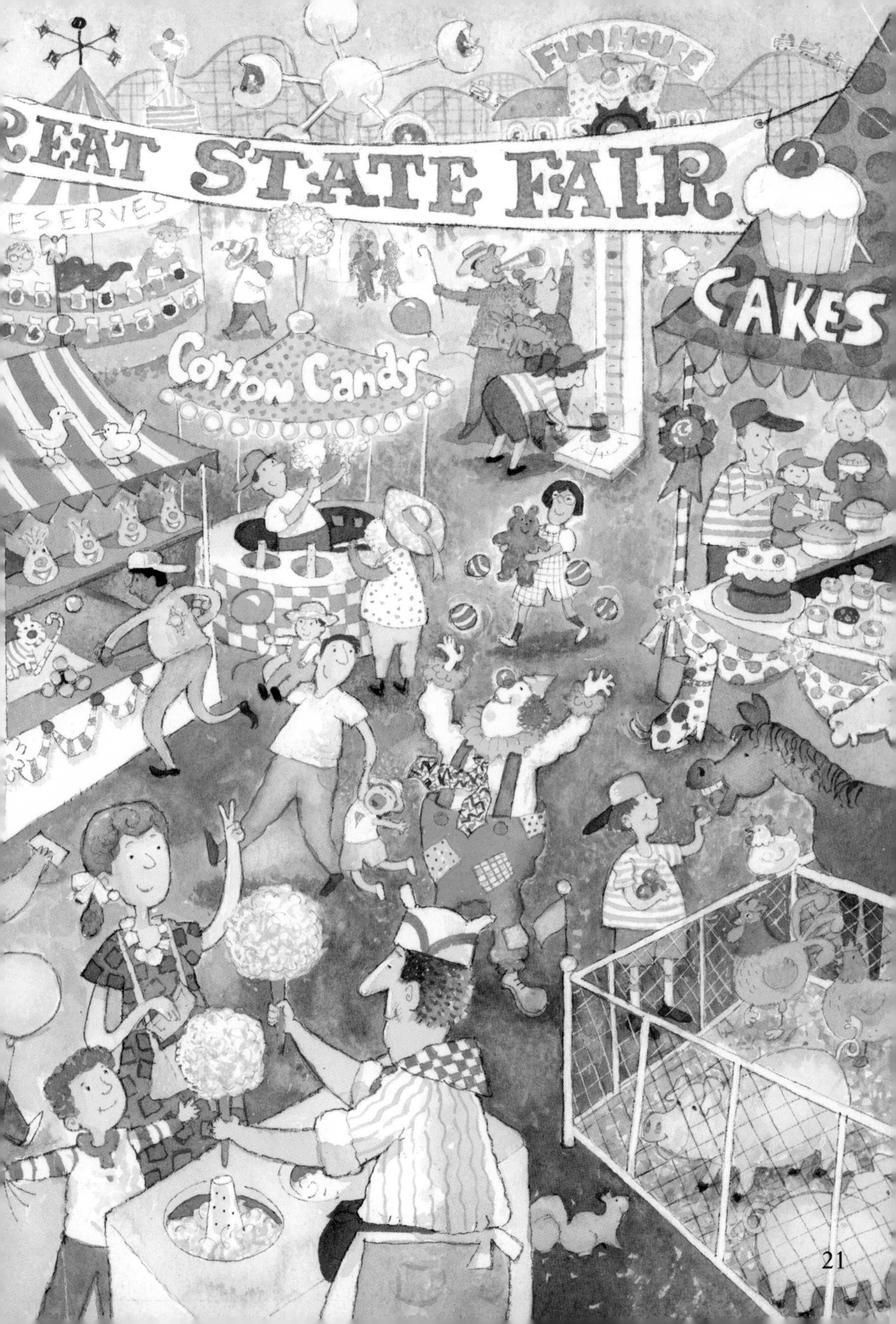
FUN HOUSE
REAT STATE FAIR
ESERVES
Cotton Candy
CAKES

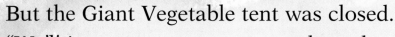

But the Giant Vegetable tent was closed.

"We'll just get some cotton candy and come back later," said Gram.

"We can't," Jay told her. "Our trolley leaves at 1:30."

"Oh, no! I wanted to see the giant jalapeño!" Gram looked very disappointed.

GREAT STATE FAIR TROLLEY SCHEDULE
Saturday & Sunday

Departs Station	Arrives at Fair	Departs Fair	Arrives at Station
10:00 A.M.	10:30 A.M.	10:30 A.M.	11:00 A.M.
11:00 A.M.	11:30 A.M.	11:30 A.M.	12:00 P.M.
12:00 P.M.	12:30 P.M.	12:30 P.M.	1:00 P.M.
1:00 P.M.	1:30 P.M.	1:30 P.M.	2:00 P.M.
2:00 P.M.	2:30 P.M.	2:30 P.M.	3:00 P.M.
3:00 P.M.	3:30 P.M.	3:30 P.M.	4:00 P.M.

"Wait, Jay!" said Kit. She took the schedule and flipped it over. "You're reading the Monday to Friday side. Today's Saturday. We can get a trolley at 2:30 and still be back in time to catch our train."

Jay stared at her. Then he checked the schedule for himself. "I can't believe it," he murmured. "You're right, Kit!"

Gram whooped. "Jalapeño, here we come!"

There was lots to do while they waited.

At 12:00 they heard a champion hog-caller.

At 12:45 Gram decided to enter a pie-eating contest. She came in second!

At 1:30 it was time to see the giant vegetables. They *were* amazing. First prize went to a radish as big as a beach ball. Gram, Kit, and Jay had their picture taken with it.

At 2:30 they took the trolley back to the station. And at 3:30 they got on their new train.

The train stopped in Sunny City, Florida, at 4:45. It was cloudy. Jay and Kit met their parents at the Sunny Suites Inn—just as it started to rain.

Train 24 ❋ Corndale to Blue Water

S A T U R D A Y	Corndale, FL	Depart	3:30 P.M.
	Sunny City, FL	Arrive	4:45 P.M.
		Depart	5:00 P.M.
	Blue Water, FL	Arrive	6:00 P.M.

Before the kids went to bed that night,
Gram said, "The wedding's at 10:00 tomorrow.
When should we be ready to leave, Jay?"

"We'll be fine if we're out the door at 9:30—
on the dot." He glanced at Kit.

"Not a problem," she said.

The next morning, Jay woke up to a loud
thumping noise. Drum? No. Stampede? No.
He looked around. The sun was so bright
outside! *What time was it?*

"Jay?" Kit called. She thumped on his door
again. "Jay! Wake up!"

Jay bolted out of bed. "Why didn't my alarm clock go off?"

"Relax," Kit said. "It's still early. The rain last night made the power go out. No alarms rang."

Jay blinked. "So how come *you're* awake?"

"Magic," she said, grinning. "The clock Hector and Bob gave me works on batteries! Now, let's wake everyone up. We don't want to be late for the wedding, do we?"

And thanks to Kit, they weren't.

SCHEDULES

Can you read down? Can you read across?
Great! Then you can read a train schedule!

Suppose you want to take the Beach Express from Shell Town to Dolphin Bay. You want to depart on Friday and arrive on Saturday.

THE BEACH EXPRESS RAILWAY SCHEDULE

TRAIN 15 ✳ Castle Side to Dolphin Bay

Step 1: Read down to find Friday and across for Shell Town.	F R I D A Y	Castle Side	Depart	5:30 P.M.
		Shell Town	Arrive	6:00 P.M.
Step 2: Find Depart. Then read across to see what time the train leaves.			Depart	6:15 P.M.
		Sunnyvale	Arrive	9:00 P.M.
			Depart	10:00 P.M.
Step 3: Read down to find Saturday and across for Dolphin Bay.	S A T U R D A Y	Sailor Cove	Arrive	6:00 A.M.
			Depart	6:05 A.M.
		Lighthouse	Arrive	8:30 A.M.
Step 4: Find Arrive. Then read across to find the time the train gets to Dolphin Bay.			Depart	9:00 A.M.
		Dolphin Bay	Arrive	10:00 A.M.

Answer the following questions about your trip.
1. On which day will you leave?
2. From which town will you leave?
3. At what time does the train depart?
4. On which day will your train ride end?
5. In which city will it end?
6. At what time will you get to your destination?

Answers: 1. Friday, 2. Shell Town, 3. 6:15 P.M., 4. Saturday, 5. Dolphin Bay, 6. 10:00 A.M.